Calling All Lovers

Calling All Lovers

Harmony Lynn

© 2020 by Harmony Lynn

All rights reserved. This book or any portion thereof may not be reproduced or used in any manner whatsoever with the express written permission of the publisher except for the use of brief quotations in a book review.

ISBN: 9798656183796

NOTE:

Names and identifying details have been changed to protect the individuals' privacy.

Chapter 1
Hey, Lovers

Hey, lovers. I'm Tessa. We just met, and we already have something in common: *love*. We've all loved someone with every inch of ourselves before. We've done things out of love that we can't even believe. This love that I want to tell you about, it consumed me. It made me happy yet sad. It made me feel stupid, yet I became wiser. This love made me hopeful yet miserable. I haven't met anyone whose situation ended up like mine, but I'm glad I can share my story with each of you.

It took so long for me to get over this love. The wound may heal, but there is an ugly scar left behind. Lovers, I'm not sure if you're still in the relationship that made you feel this way or not, but I hope after reading this, you realize your worth and make a decision to honor that worth moving forward. I hope that knowing you are not alone in how you feel gives you the courage to share your story and be completely honest about it. Honesty is one of the hardest things to give to someone and one of the hardest things to receive.

I am here to help anyone who's ever loved someone that just couldn't love them back the same way. I want you to know that it's okay to admit how badly this love hurt you. This love broke you into pieces. It broke your confidence, your self-esteem. It killed your fairy-tale dream of true love, but lovers, even after all of that, you can love again. You can regain your confidence, your self-esteem, and even your fairy-tale. Love knows no skin color, race, or gender—love is for all.

Tell me something: How much time have you spent wondering why you let the person you fell so deeply in love with mistreat you? If you're anything like me, you've spent weeks, months, even years. You've told your best friend that you're done over a dozen times, but then you always circle back to the fact that you love them. Once you have history with someone, you don't want to give up on them. You don't want to lose your fairy-tale ending. You want to be that long-term couple everyone looks up to and who makes them wish they could find a love like yours. Well, lovers, the time came when I had to face it. It was time to mend my broken heart, to heal the bruises to my self-esteem, and to shine like the star I was born to be. It's time for you to shine, love. Past time.

Chapter 2
Just Kids

I remember the first time I laid eyes on Jesse. It was during my lunch period in junior high. Each of the three grades had separate lunch periods. I never believed in love at first sight, but this had to be it. My heart started racing. My palms were sweaty, and I just couldn't keep still.

"Who is *that*?" I was trying to see around the large cafeteria crowd without being too obvious.

"I think his name is Jesse. He just transferred here," a voice said.

He was standing in the doorway of the cafeteria, waiting for the bell to ring. I had never seen a boy so beautiful before.

"Can someone go talk to him for me, please?" I exclaimed. I was too nervous to do it myself.

My friends laughed. "You need to calm down. Are you okay?"

"He is so fine."

I should have known from that moment that I was in for

heartbreak. Our obvious age difference didn't bother me. He was in the sixth grade, but his height made that hard to believe, and I was in eighth. All I wanted was him. No matter what.

According to my parents, I was too young to date, but I was heading into high school the next year. I didn't want to miss my chance, so I put my friends to work.

"Tyra, do you have any classes with him?" I asked. "Who are his friends? I need info!"

Allison said casually, "He lives on Brush Lane, I think. I see him walking home every day."

This was it. This was going to be the way to let him know I was interested. I was too shy to talk to him myself. Fear of being rejected. Now that I think about it, everybody did it this way in junior high. No one talked to anyone on their own first. They used a friend. I wasn't the most popular girl in school. I didn't have the nicest clothes or shoes. To be honest, he seemed way cooler than me. But after all the digging my friends did for me, we exchanged numbers and started talking. I couldn't believe it! My generation called this "going together." I couldn't wait to tell my friends.

The morning bell rang at 8:10 a.m., telling us that class was going to start in twenty minutes. As I was getting my things out of my locker, I heard Tyra and Allison running up behind me. They both hit the lockers so hard that you could hear the sound at the end of the hall. "So what happened? Do you guys go together or not?" they both yelled.

I couldn't help but blush. "Yes, ma'am!" I said. They high-fived me as if I'd just announced I'd won something big. "I'm going to give him a hug today at lunch when I see him." So sweet and innocent.

See, lovers, I was convinced that he was my first love, and nothing could come between us. I know it might sound crazy that, at age fourteen, I felt so strongly for someone. Especially when the *going together* phase ended up being so short lived. He called me one evening about a month later just to say, "I don't want to go with you anymore." I was shocked, to say the least, but what else could I say besides okay? Anger quickly set in. I hadn't done anything wrong. Why was this happening? Little did I know, the gossip at school the next day would reveal the truth.

Her name was Taylor. One of the prettiest girls I'd ever seen. I definitely didn't feel that I measured up. She and her sister were new students from the other side of town. Their parents had recently moved into the neighborhood. I don't think two full days had gone by since their joining the school before I heard the news that Taylor and Jesse were a couple. Right here, in this very moment, is where the pattern of Jesse's behavior over the course of our young lives began. This is where I went wrong. I accepted being his second choice. For years to come, he always had a number one pick, and I was always number two. Soon after Taylor moved on, I got word that Jesse wanted to get back with me. I was still so captivated by him that I accepted. We were young. I didn't know anything about my worth or that I was actually being mistreated.

I mean, after all, there was nothing to our relationship besides telephone conversations and hugs. No arguments or anything negative, really. We seemed to be just good friends who happened to like each other.

Jesse had big dreams. He wanted to be a sports agent. He could have been a professional athlete himself. He knew a lot about sports—football, basketball, soccer, and track and field. You name it, he knew it. His dreams called for him to travel to different sporting events on the weekends. Long days, late nights, tournaments, scrimmages, and summer leagues. I waited. I waited for his call, his text, his page. You know, back then we had pagers. It was like a one-way text message, except you could only send your number and wait for the person to call you. It didn't matter what time it was. I was waiting. One Friday night he paged me, and when I called him back, he asked to see me.

"You know it's the middle of the night, right?" I said.

"Just sneak out of the house. I'll meet you at the corner."

I was terrified. What if my parents caught me? What if the police stopped me? But it was Jesse, and I missed him. I quickly got dressed and eased down the stairs. Not too many people had house alarms the way they do now, so I didn't have to deal with that. Once I made it out, I nearly ran to the corner. I must have looked back fifteen times to see if I noticed any movement or lights at home. I actually made it! Late-night visits became our thing that summer. Thankfully, I quit walking to meet him. I convinced him to just come over. We would sit on the front porch and just be together. Talk, laugh, make up games to play with one another. He fell asleep as I held him in my arms a few times. I remember thinking that I must be the luckiest girl in the world. Of all the places he could be, all the girls he could have been with, he chose to be with me. Those summer nights were everything to me.

Chapter 3
High School, Not Sweethearts

It was my senior year of high school, and we were so far away from each other that we decided to just be friends. His parents had sent him to boarding school, and we didn't want the distance to be too much on us. It was his suggestion, but I went with it. There were times where we didn't communicate as often, and this left nothing but opportunity to get to know other people.

During my four years, I had two boyfriends and my first kiss, but nothing serious. I was all about Jesse. I was just waiting for the right time for us to be together. I had no idea he was off growing up way faster than I was. I don't know who his first time was with, but it wasn't me. I was fine with it, because I had decided that I was waiting until at least after high school. I could see and hear how the *active girls* were treated and talked about in school, and I didn't want that for myself. Yes, I hoped it would be with a special someone who loved me, and I loved him, but it turned out he was very nonspecial, and we did not love each other. It happened shortly after graduation. He was from another school. It honestly was nothing special, which I regret, but you live and you learn. All I cared about was that it was summer again.

Summertime allowed Jesse and me to see each other more. But this summer would be different, because I had to leave for culinary school in August. I was pursuing a fast-track degree where I had to go to school year-round for one year and then do an externship for three months. I wasn't sure if we would still communicate. I wasn't sure how often I would come home. A part of me wished that I didn't have to go.

This particular summer wasn't too different from the others, except Jesse's friend Anthony hung out with us a lot. Anthony was super cool and so funny. He was always rooting for Jesse and me to make it. He used to call me Jesse's real girlfriend. In a way I thought that maybe he knew more about Jesse's feelings and intentions toward me than I did, and that was why he gave me that title. Anthony's voice used to be really high, so he would always call and ask for me because I wasn't allowed to talk to boys. Jesse used three-way calling to get us connected, and then Anthony would hang up. Anyway, the three of us had fun together. Anthony was always with Jesse. At each other's homes, at the gym, sporting events, and camps. I may have been a little jealous at times, but he was his best friend. He would always be able to go places that I couldn't go with Jesse. Anthony didn't go to Jesse's boarding school though; he went to my high school. He may have been how Jesse kept tabs on me, ha!

Anthony didn't come over with Jesse on my last night in town. Jesse came alone. We talked for hours. I should have spent a lot of that time packing, but boys definitely weren't allowed in my room for me to be able to multitask. I felt the need to explain how much I loved him and wanted to be with him. I even said I'd marry him if he asked! I had just turned eighteen! What was I thinking? Looking back on it, I feel that I was too vocal about my feelings. I smothered him with how I felt, but when you feel a certain way about someone and you've never felt that way before, it almost forces you to tell them. You feel like you'll explode if you don't. He didn't propose, of course, but he understood how I felt. When it was time to say goodbye, we did so with a kiss and the longest hug in history. I didn't want to let go. But life moves on, and so did he.

The first couple of months away weren't too bad. We called, we texted, but it didn't last long. He was still in boarding school and had a lot on his plate. He made a lot of connections through his school that would later help him with his career aspirations. He was always traveling. I didn't want to be too clingy or too needy, so I chose to take a back seat. He knew where to find me if he wanted to. It wasn't long before I found out he had a girlfriend. Brooke was her name. She was also a student at my high school. Same grade as Jesse. I knew exactly who she was. She was short with a thick build and long dark hair, her complexion a little lighter than caramel. She was a senior and had been set up with Jesse by Anthony. Anthony was Jesse's wingman, and I couldn't fault him for that. I only wondered how the distance between them was so easy to overcome. It was literally the same distance that he suggested would be too much for us. How could she be the girlfriend, but he just wanted to be friends with me? It didn't seem fair—and it wasn't. Not to me, at least. But I chose to keep playing my friend role. I chose to communicate with him no matter what, because that's what *friends* do, right?

The term "friend" can be misinterpreted between men and women a lot of times. Not everyone trusts that a friend is only a friend. Brooke was interested in finding out for herself just how friendly Jesse and I were after she went through Jesse's phone and didn't like what she saw. She went so far as to create a bogus story to feed to Jesse just to get away with going through his phone.

Jesse called me, saying, "I don't really know what's going on, but Brooke said someone gave her your number and told her she was in for a rude awakening."

I was not interested in being in the middle of anybody's drama. Especially over a *friend*. I couldn't think of anyone who would do that, but that's what she told him. His call to me was to simply cover his tracks. He had the audacity to give me instructions: "If she calls you, you don't know me."

I was in such disbelief at what he said. *"Huh?"*

"Act like you don't know me. You don't know my name or anything."

"Okay, sure," I replied. I was so pissed and so done all at the same time. How could he treat me like this? Better yet, why was he treating me like this? We were just friends, and nothing was happening between us! See, when your lover is or feels guilty, they will go to great lengths to cover their tracks.

I was ready for Brooke when she called. Ready to deny whatever she thought she knew. I had no interest in telling her anything, because there was nothing to tell.

She seemed so sweet and innocent on the phone. I really believe she was just trying to figure out what the hell was going on with her man. It wasn't long before her cover was blown. The little plan she'd cooked up with her best friend, Dana, was discovered by Dana's boyfriend, Kyle. Did I mention that Kyle knew Jesse? They'd played sports together in junior high. Uh oh! Silly rabbit! It was the dumbest plan ever, lovers! Kyle called Jesse and told him everything. This left Jesse with his tail between his legs.

He called me to ask if we could meet to talk. "About what?" I asked. There was nothing but attitude in my voice.

"Please." It was a word I had never heard him say and with such sincerity. I was still a sucker for him and for every sweet word that he uttered.

"Fine, when?"

"Tomorrow night."

I agreed. I was still upset with him, but I wanted to hear what he had to say. After all, he had never used those words before—"can we talk." It was very grown up for him.

You know I had to make sure I was extra cute for this talk, right? Hair done, tight jeans, cute top. I was ready. When he showed up, he suggested that we take a walk.

"Walk where? It's already nine o'clock at night."

"Walk with me to Anthony's house." I had never been to Anthony's house, but it wasn't too far away. The entire walk over there, he made small talk. I didn't pry, because I could tell he was nervous. I wasn't used to this behavior from him. We joked and reminisced about a few memories we shared. It was nice. He must've needed the time it took to walk over there to build up the nerve to say what he had to say. We finally arrived at Anthony's and sat down on the porch.

"Are you ready to talk now?" I asked. "What's on your mind, Jesse?"

He took a deep breath and looked me straight in the eyes. "That stuff with Brooke was really messed up, and I want to apologize for it. I shouldn't have asked you to lie, and you shouldn't have been in the middle of that. I apologize."

Oh my God, lovers! When someone has wronged you and they realize it on their own and offer you an apology on their own—that is major! I had nothing but respect for him in that moment. I was so appreciative. I accepted his apology, and we hugged. Although we were friends, I felt that maybe we were laying the foundation for something more. Once his relationship with Brooke ended, he said he needed time. I was willing to wait as long as I had to.

Chapter 4
From Rags to Rich's

Once I finished my year of culinary school, I was lucky enough to return home for my externship at a five-star hotel in downtown Cleveland. I hoped that by now Jesse had taken all the time he needed and wanted to get back together, but he wanted to remain friends. What else is new, right? As a young woman going into her twenties, I started to crave the attention of a man who was willing to show me some. I wanted a real relationship, because technically I had never had one. There just so happened to be a very cute guy working as a steward at the hotel. Rich was his name. I could tell he was a bad boy. His initials were tattooed on his neck, and he just had that vibe, you know? We had only said hello and have a good day to each other, but one day he decided to start a different conversation. One that included asking me my age and if I had a boyfriend.

I answered both questions honestly. "I am nineteen, and no, I don't."

He was twenty-two years old. I'm not sure how I knew, but

I knew this would be a completely new experience for me. He offered to take me home from work sometime. I declined the offer out of fear several times. My mother always said to be careful with people you don't really know. Rich had a beautiful smile and an infectious laugh. One day I accepted his offer for the ride home. I let my parents know that I would be getting a ride home from someone at work. I didn't learn to drive until the next year, so I always took the bus and a train to get to and from work.

The night I accepted Rich's offer, he said he'd wait for me by the exit. We both had to change out of the hotel uniforms and into our plain clothes. He was even cuter in his polo shirt, fitted jeans, and sneakers. The ride home was surprisingly quiet. It was like that awkward moment that you realize you like each other, but because you just met, you don't know what to do or say. I was nervous. I thought this could be the start of something serious. Something I never had. A relationship that would involve more than just conversations on my front porch or a walk around the block. More than just a hug and kiss. I wasn't sure that I was ready for something like that. A part of me wanted to always be available when Jesse decided he was ready, but why should I put my life on hold? Maybe Rich was everything I had been looking for. I wasn't sure what was going to happen between us, but I was ready to get to know him better.

I didn't tell Jesse about Rich, because I didn't need to. He never told me about his girlfriends. I'd met a guy who was into me. That's not exactly the type of thing Jesse and I would discuss. Deep down I felt like I was caught between two people. It was no secret that my heart longed for Jesse, but I liked Rich. He was a fresh start. I had to know how Jesse felt before I could make any decisions about Rich. During a conversation with Jesse, he revealed the news of having a girlfriend. This one was named Alexus. She fit the description of a thick redbone. She was about five two, and we couldn't have been more opposites of each other. He posted their picture on his social media account. She looked so cozy sitting on his lap as they posed for the camera. It was one of those pictures that just screamed, "He's all mine." Looking at it made me feel sadness and confusion. Whenever I asked him why we couldn't be together, he always answered, "I'm not ready for a relationship right now." Lovers, I don't know why I couldn't get it through my head that he didn't want me. He was always showing me that, but I didn't want to face it.

"Oh, so you have a girlfriend, Jesse?" My emotions wouldn't let it rest without an explanation, but I didn't want to seem angry, so I had to remain calm.

"Yeah, I do."

"What happened to not being ready for a relationship though?" I was becoming more and more pissed off.

"I mean, it just kind of happened…and you and I are just friends, I thought." His nonchalant demeanor was so obvious.

You know that moment when all you want to do is explode in anger and start yelling? Well, this was my moment. I just wanted to scream out, "Because that's what *you* wanted!" but my pride wouldn't let me do it. I couldn't let him see me sweat. All I could say was, "Oh, okay. I'm happy for you." He tried to slip a joke in before the conversation ended, just to get an idea of how pissed I really was, but I couldn't even laugh. I was numb. I felt so stupid. He had literally done this right under my nose. I spent the rest of the night blaming myself and listening to sad love songs. We weren't together. How could I be angry? He wasn't mine. He hadn't cheated on me. Yet I was angry and felt that I *had* been cheated on. Even though I was hurt, I justified his behavior. I had known him the longest, and he kept coming back to me. That had to mean something. I must've meant something to him; otherwise he would just leave me alone, right? I was being forced to move on, and who better to move on with than Rich? I wanted to give Rich and me a real chance, which meant I had to disconnect myself from Jesse. I never thought I would ever disconnect myself from him, but he had played me like a fool too many times. He wasn't the only one who could find another someone.

Chapter 5
Baby Blues

Rich was proving to be more of a man than Jesse, and he was more into me, all of me—my milk-chocolate complexion, slim build, big smile, even bigger laugh, and sensitivity. We had fun together. We had been dating for seven months, and we actually went on dates. Unlike Jesse, who had never taken me anywhere. Rich and I went to the movies, restaurants, miniature golf, concerts, festivals, and so on. He enjoyed spending time with me and I with him. I was happy to be Rich's girlfriend. I had nothing to lose. When Jesse would text to say, "Hey, what's up," all he got in return were one-word answers—"nothing," "yeah," "okay." I was bitter towards him. I was fine right where I was, so why did he need to check on me? No, thanks. Then one day my cell phone rang while I was at work. An unknown number. I remember thinking, "Whoever this is must really need to talk to me, because they keep calling!" So I answered.

"Hello!"

A female voice that I didn't recognize responded, "Yeah,

hello."

"Hello?" Who could this be on my phone? I wondered. Then she said, "Who is this?"

"You called me. Who are you?" I could feel myself getting defensive.

"This is Alexus, and I'm just trying to figure out why your number is in my boyfriend's phone."

I was instantly aggravated. "Girl, please, that is a grown man who's going to do what he wants to do, so if you want to know something, ask him!" *Click!* Hell yeah, I hung up on her. She had no business calling me. Her issue was with her boyfriend, not me. I spent the rest of the day telling my friends Tyra and Allison about my dose of drama, but before the night was over, the drama continued. It must have been around eleven o'clock when Jesse called. I was laughing when I answered, because I just knew he was going to say something stupid.

"Ah, man, what's up, Jesse?"

"Why are you laughing?"

"What can I do for you?" My attitude was setting in. I didn't have time for the BS. He went on to ask me what happened when Alexus called, and I told him word for word.

"Did you tell her anything?"

"About what?"

According to Jesse, his girlfriend had made up her own version of what happened. One that included me telling her that I could have him if I wanted him and that she didn't mean anything to him. I couldn't believe he was calling to check me.

Me! I hadn't called his girlfriend, and I would never say anything like that. I thought he knew me better than that.

"Look, Jesse, just go talk to your girlfriend. She's the one who needs answers."

Months went by without any calls or texts from Jesse. Thank goodness. Rich and I were still going strong. I started using my time wisely. Outside of my relationship with Rich, I worked a corporate job downtown and spent time with my girls. I had to learn to take care of myself. No time to worry about anyone who wasn't worried about me.

Just after leaving work one day, I received a text from Allison that read, CALL ME ASAP. This made me nervous. You never know what will come after a text like that.

"Allison, what happened? What's wrong?"

She hesitantly said to me, "Tess, he has a baby on the way."

"Who?" Hoping that I didn't know the answer.

"Jesse!"

I felt the tears building up and ready to fall down my face. "With Alexus?"

"Yes, girl."

I just cried. I sat in my car and cried. I never saw that coming. Then the love I had for him made me feel a way that I don't think anyone else would feel in this moment: I felt like he needed a friend. I needed to make sure he was okay. I couldn't call, because I didn't want him to know that I was crying, so I sent a text: Jesse, is she pregnant? He responded: I guess so. I just told him that I hoped she and the baby were okay and that I was here if he needed me. I wanted him to know that I cared. Most importantly I wanted him to see that I was there for him no matter what. How could he not make his way back to someone who was willing to care for him through something like this?

Sending my support reopened the door for communication, general hellos and how are you. I let him know I had a boyfriend. He said he was happy for me. I really hoped he was just a little bit jealous, but I had no way of knowing if he was. He didn't seem to care. I always asked about the baby until one day he called and said, "Tessa, she's so grimy! I swear I don't want anybody but you!"

My heart melted, but my mind was so confused by such a sudden change of heart. "Jesse, what happened?" I asked, over and over again. "Tell me what's wrong, please."

He said in a loud voice, *"She's not even pregnant!"*

She had lied. Who does that? Why would she put him through that? I felt so sorry for him, but I also felt relieved. This person that could've kept us from getting back together was gone, and he wanted me. He'd come back to me. Thank you, God! Then I remembered. What about Rich? My mind flooded with thoughts. I couldn't leave Rich. He had been there for me. He had been sweet to me. He could be falling in love with me. As much as it hurt me, I told Jesse I couldn't be with him and that I needed time. A part of me was being vengeful, but I could not hurt Rich. He didn't deserve that. Jesse understood. After all, I had waited years for him.

Chapter 6
Cheaters Never Prosper

A feeling I will never forget is betrayal. The kind when a man cheats on a woman. I don't think I ever tried to imagine what it would feel like if I found out someone was cheating on me. I knew that it had happened to different women in my life, and it was hard on them. Now it was my turn.

I trusted Rich. Our issues started about a year into our relationship. He decided he wanted more from me. When I say more, I mean he wanted a child. Lovers, please understand me when I say this: all over the world, there are couples who can sit down and discuss a life-changing event like this and come to an agreement to have a child together. Congratulations to them. More power and blessing to them. I am *not* the one, however.

I grew up feeling the need to be as perfect as I could be in the sight of my parents, whom I adored. I wanted to get married and then have children. I was not wavering. No man could talk me into having a baby when I wasn't ready. I wanted to have a home of my own with my husband before bringing an innocent child into the picture. I wanted my last name to be the same as my child's last name. This issue caused Rich and me to do a lot of breaking up and making up. He didn't want to lose me, but he also wanted to see what else was out there. I had a gut feeling that something was going on, but I actually let his words make me believe something different. Then one day I went to check the time on his phone and saw a name on the screen: Tiffany.

"Who is Tiffany?" I asked.

"Oh, she's a friend of mine."

I didn't read into it at the time, because I believe that all things will be revealed when they need to be. A few weeks later, while I was sitting at the front desk at work, my cell phone rang. Repeatedly. They called so many times that I decided to call the number back from my desk phone. A woman answered.

"Yes, this is Tessa, and someone keeps calling me from this number."

"This is Tiffany. Do you know who I am?"

"Um, a friend of Rich's, right?"

She snickered. "If you want to call it that. I've been seeing him for about three months now, and we've been sleeping together. He took me to Georgia to meet his mom last month and everything."

Clearly, I was a magnet for taking calls from another woman. I never felt the need to call another woman to talk about a man. I didn't understand why, yet again, a female was calling me about a man. Needless to say, I was stunned. I couldn't believe what I was hearing. I told Tiffany that I would call her back, because I was at work, and she clearly had more to say. As I headed toward the ladies' room, I grabbed my coworker and friend, Kelly. Before I could make it into the restroom, I just broke down. I mean *completely* broke down. Sobbing in Kelly's arms, I could barely speak. It took me a few minutes to get myself together and tell Kelly what happened. Kelly tried consoling me. She said that this is what men do. They cheat. And it's not just men who cheat. Women do too. After I calmed down, I called Rich and told him what happened. He spent most of the time asking me what Tiffany had said rather than denying it or apologizing. He was trying to find out how much she'd told me and to regain control of the situation, but he couldn't. Once two women begin to tell each other the dirty secrets of a man who's trying to creep, it's a wrap!

After work that night, I called Tiffany back. I wanted to hear what else she had to say. She knew about conversations that Rich and I had, because she'd been with him at the time that we had them. She had indeed been to Georgia to meet his family—it was the trip that I couldn't make due to work, so he'd taken her instead. I had been to Georgia with Rich before, though, so when Tiffany described the layout of his mother's home, I knew she was telling the truth. Tiffany described his apartment, his bedroom, and the photos he had up of us. I started to recall all the moments that my intuition had told me something was up—his words that seemed like lies, his actions that felt secretive, all of it. I should have known something was up, but I'd ignored the signs. Now I was stuck feeling stupid, ashamed, and embarrassed. After two years of our back and forth, this was how it ended. Just as I thought we were done with the arguing and that we were actually trying to work on getting back together for real.

Having to explain to my family why all of a sudden they would never see Rich again was the worst part. I never thought this would happen to me. To be honest, I'd tried to imagine what it would be like, but what I didn't expect was to have to know the woman, talk to her, hear her tell me how she'd literally taken my place. This was a hard pill to swallow. I had so much anger inside that I disconnected myself from everyone around me. I was mean as hell. All because I didn't know how to really express myself to those around me and didn't know how to deal with my anger.

I cried so much over Rich. Actually, I cried because I was smart enough to see what was happening but had been blinded by the trust I had for him. It took a while to feel normal again. I spent a lot of time alone. I'll never forget going to the movies to see *Dear John* by myself. I knew it was going to make me cry, and I didn't want anyone to see me. I was in a bad place, but the movie made me wish I had Jesse to wipe my tears away and tell me he loved me. But I had no one.

Chapter 7
He Loves Me, Not

After a few months of what I now know was depression, I was able to get myself together and start spending time with my girls again. The new girl at work, Marie, had been asking me to hang out. We were the same age, and she was really sweet. The more we hung out, the closer we became. Summer was around the corner, and we were both turning into party animals. There was a club to go to every Thursday, Friday, Saturday, and Sunday! It wasn't often, but we definitely hit up all four clubs in a weekend. We were young, single, and beautiful. We were having so much fun! The promoters were friends of Jesse's, so we started running into him at the clubs. It was difficult trying to explain to Marie how I was in love with a person who didn't want to be with me, and with whom I hadn't been in a relationship with *titles* since grade school. Hell, it didn't make any sense to me either, but it was the truth. I tried not to speak a few times, but Jesse wasn't going to let that happen. He would come say hello and give me a hug. Lovers, have you ever wanted to push someone away from you and hug them at the same time? That's how I felt every time I saw him out! Seeing each other led to text messages, phone conversations, and eventually spending time together again.

He asked me to come over to his sister's place one night after work. She worked a lot, so he always had the place to himself. I remember it like it was yesterday. I wore a blue denim skirt and white tank top. I made sure to wear a sweet-smelling perfume and the perfect lip gloss, and my hair was freshly done. I thought I was cute. When I arrived, he greeted me with a hug. He was wearing a pair of black-and-red basketball shorts and no shirt! In my head I was already five steps ahead of him. He asked if I wanted to watch a comedy show. "Sure, why not," I replied.

The vibe was super cool. Our energy was in sync. We laughed, and he held me close to him on the couch as we watched. It felt so good to be next to him. There was a moment where he made a joke, and as we laughed, we turned to each other. It felt like a scene from your favorite romance movie where things get intense quickly—and then, we kissed. The rest was history. The dynamics of our relationship had finally changed after that night. It felt like we were taking the steps to become a couple in serious relationship.

We began spending even more time together. Real time. Dates. Time that included our families. As an only child, I didn't have siblings to fight with growing up, but I did have close cousins. My closest cousin was Chase. We were a few years apart, but we shared a lot of the same characteristics. Chase was a ladies' man. Handsome, cool, funny, and charming. Everyone knew him. He worked very hard all of our younger years, because he knew he was going to be famous. He devoted his life to the sport of football. Everything in his life revolved around it, so I wasn't surprised when he and Jesse hit it off. A sports agent and an athlete—their conversations went on for hours sometimes, which was fine with me, because at least it was still time we spent together. Then Jesse and Chase started hanging out a little, going to the gym or to catch a game at the bar. It didn't bother me until I started seeing less and less of Jesse. He was up to his old tricks again. He started standing me up, making excuses, lying, not answering my calls as much. If I let my number show when I called, he wouldn't answer, but if I blocked it or called from a number that he didn't know, he'd answer by the second ring. Lovers, how dumb is that? Obviously, if someone is trying to call you repeatedly and then you get a call from a blocked number, it's probably them! I never said a word when he answered. I would just hang up. He would even call back sometimes if it was just a different number. To this day, I've never met anyone so bothered by me that they wouldn't take my call. It hurt my feelings a little, but I was unknowingly becoming numb to the hurt he caused. I was building a wall to cover up how I really felt and to keep myself from getting hurt more. All I needed was for him to be honest with me about what he wanted. Whether it hurt me or not, I would have respected his honesty, and I would have left him alone. That constant need to know had me doing things that really made me look and feel foolish. I eventually just gave up. I was tired of using my energy for someone who didn't even want to take my calls.

A few weeks later, Chase and I decided to grab dinner and catch up. When Chase walked in, he was laughing on the phone as his call ended.

"What's so funny?"

"Jesse was just telling me this funny story."

I think my face turned to stone for a few seconds. "So you guys are like real live friends now?"

He gave me a quick response. "I mean, we cool."

My entire mood changed. How could my best friend and family—someone who was so close to me that we were like siblings—become friends with someone who broke my heart every chance he got? I wasn't having it!

"I'm not comfortable with that, Chase."

"Why though?" He seemed so confused.

"He should not be allowed to hang with you and be all buddy-buddy and then treat me any kind of way at the same time." I realized that my voice had gotten loud.

Chase made a comment that he wouldn't let anyone do me wrong, but then he changed the subject of the conversation so fast that I knew he was trying to avoid talking about it anymore. I was becoming more upset. Although Chase was like a brother to me, we never talked about anything serious. We kept our conversations light and funny. The time we spent together was mostly about having fun and making each other laugh. We might have suffered some losses together, but he was always the person to make everyone laugh when they felt like crying. I wanted to continue the conversation, but I could tell he didn't. It killed me to know that I had so much to say about how I felt, but I didn't think it would make a difference. I just stuffed the feelings down and tried my best not to let it bother me.

I needed something to take my mind off things. My birthday was coming up, and I decided to throw myself a party. My birthday was a big deal every year, but that year I was turning twenty-two, and I wanted to celebrate myself. I wanted to get a fancy dress and fancy shoes, get all dolled up, and party all day and night! I planned a party at a local bistro and had my parents, aunts, and older cousins party with me earlier in the evening. Then my close friends and younger cousins joined me later that same night. It was awesome!

Marie kept telling me that Jesse was coming. I told her there was no way, because I didn't invite him. I hadn't talked to him in a few weeks, and it felt kind of normal. I didn't want to worry about if he was going to show up or not. I wanted everything to be about me. As I headed to the dance floor, I looked up, and Jesse was walking toward me. Marie jumped up, dancing and celebrating the fact that she was right. For a split second, I didn't know how to feel. I wasn't sure what his presence meant. He walked up and gave me a hug as usual. He always had the ability to act like nothing had happened. Like I wasn't mad at him. It might have put a smile on my face, but I still asked him what he was doing there.

He replied, "What do you mean? You thought I wasn't going to come? I mean, you didn't invite me, but it's cool. Chase mentioned it." Everything was always cool. I had so much to say, but my birthday party definitely wasn't the place.

"We should get together and talk soon, Jesse." He agreed. He didn't stay at the party long. He said he had to pick up Anthony. We made plans to meet up and talk in a few days. For me, this was the single most important thing on my mind. By Tuesday, I was already anxious. I reached out to see what day would work for him. We settled on Wednesday evening. All day Wednesday I went over what I wanted to say a million times. I knew that this conversation would basically make or break us forever. I decided not to text or call all day on Wednesday. I wanted to see if this was something that he was actually going to follow through with. I wondered if this was a priority to him. The sun was going down. Seven o'clock came, eight o'clock, nine. By ten o'clock I was fed up. Why couldn't he just do right for once? Why show up to my party only to stand me up a few days later? I reluctantly called him. I wasn't expecting him to answer, but he did. I immediately had to sound cool, calm, and collected.

"Hey, what are you doing?" I asked.

"Nothing, lying down."

"So you're standing me up?"

"No."

"Okay, so?"

"I'll be on my way in a few minutes," he said.

When he arrived, I met him outside in the driveway. He sat on the back of his car while I stood in front of him.

"So what's up?" he asked.

"That's what I'm trying to figure out. We don't talk for weeks, and then you show up to my party as if everything was all good. Why do you do shit like that? You confuse the hell out of me all the time."

"I mean, I don't know what you want me to say. We're friends. I'm never the one that's mad. That's always you. I've never had an issue with you."

"Well, Jesse, I don't understand what we are or what we're doing. We've been going through this same cycle for over ten years. That's a long time to deal with someone and have it not mean anything. You know that I want to be with you, but I have no idea what you want. You act like you don't really care about my feelings at all."

He quickly replied, "That's not true."

"Then what is it? Let me know something, please."

"I just have a lot going on in my life, and I can't ask you to put your life on hold for me."

"What's going on? Tell me."

"I have an opportunity to be a scout, and I would have to relocate to Dallas for about a year."

"So I'll come with you. I'll pack my shit right now."

"I can't ask you to do that."

"You're not asking, I'm volunteering."

"Yeah, but I can't let you to do that for me."

"Then I'll wait."

"I can't ask you to do that either."

Everything I thought we were was crumbling before me. "So I should move on, is what you're saying? You just want to be friends?"

"We are friends. I just want you to be happy."

"That can't be true, because being with you is what will make me happy. But that's not what you want, right?"

"Don't say it like that."

"But that's what it is, right?"

Silence rang out for a second. The silence that proves the truth is being told, but he thought not saying it or agreeing would make it less true. I just said, "Aright, cool. Thanks for coming to talk. Get home safe." He tried making a joke as he turned to walk away, but I couldn't look at him. Tears were rolling down my face. How could our history mean so little to him? Why couldn't he see how much I loved him? I couldn't believe that this was finally the end of us. There was no way I could just be his friend. It was going to take time before I could even face him again.

I called Marie and told her it was over. He didn't want me. She asked if I was going to be okay. "Eventually," I answered. Lovers, I didn't realize at the time what I was going through. I didn't know how to get through it. Yes, the situation with Rich had been devastating, but he hadn't been a part of my life as long as Jesse. Rich hurt me on a surface level, but Jesse, he cut deep. June 11, 2008, will always be etched into my brain as the day my heart was shattered into a million pieces.

    I didn't know how to move on, really. I knew that the friendship Jesse wanted wasn't something I could give him. I didn't want to hear from him, and I didn't want to reach out to him either. Just like that, I changed my number. This was going to keep me in check about reaching out to him. As much as I didn't need any updates on him, though, they were always coming my way. Marie started a relationship with one of Jesse's other friends, so when he was scheduled to leave for Dallas, she made sure to mention it to me. There was no way I was going to see him off or anything like that. I just said a prayer for him and kept it moving. Knowing that I didn't have to see him or possibly run into him was comforting to me. I had embarrassed myself enough. I put everything into moving on. I should have put my energy into healing, but without being honest with myself about how I truly felt, I couldn't recognize that I needed to address my brokenness. I wish I'd known then what I know now; not doing the necessary work after going through that with Jesse would lead me to go about relationships the wrong way entirely. Most women wouldn't admit to a lot of what I have told you already or say what I have left to say. But I am not most women.

Chapter 8
Hey, Husband

Love sucks! That was my attitude. Love is nothing like what most people believe it is. I looked around my own family, and I saw so much love being shared between two people. A lot of different couples, from high school sweethearts to thirty-year marriages. How did they know that they had found the one? How did they make it look so effortless? I often wondered, but I never asked anyone. I just relied on believing that I would get that *special feeling*, but for the time being, I swore off dating! No dates, no phone calls, no hookups from my friends, nothing. Trying to find the perfect match after having my heart broken was exhausting just to think about. I didn't want to think about anyone or care about anyone. I just wanted to feel free.

I had a regular schedule that didn't change much: work, church, gym, and family dinner every Sunday. I occasionally went out on the weekends. I was tired of the clubs, so I started going to a place called Oasis. It was a lounge located in the lobby of a nearby hotel. Very popular place, always crowded with tons of beautiful people who were looking to have a good time without the hassle of going clubbing downtown. Oasis had easily become my favorite place to go when I wanted to let my hair down, and that was exactly what I needed after getting a call from Marie telling me Jesse had completed his job in Dallas and was coming home. His friends were throwing him a welcome-home party and wanted to be sure I was invited. *Seriously?* I thought we'd both gotten off the roller coaster before he left. Why would his friends go through all of that to make sure I was invited to his party? Had he asked for me specifically? All I knew was that I wasn't going. That year he spent in Dallas wasn't long enough for me to forget how he'd left or how he'd left me. What would I look like showing up to his party? For all I knew, he could've come back home with a girlfriend. "No, thanks," I told Marie. "I'll pass on that one."

Luckily for me my closest female cousin, Shawna, was coming to visit. Perfect timing! Shawna and I are two years apart, and I'm the older one. We were always close, but the distance sometimes made it hard for us to keep up with each other's everyday lives. She lived in Illinois. We started talking more around the time that Jesse left town, and now she was planning to visit and see the family. I knew I had to take her to my favorite place. Her trip was short, so we were forced to go out on a Thursday. Her weekend was jam-packed. To be honest I had never been to Oasis on a weekday, only Saturdays. Lovers, it was *dead*. Like only ten people in the entire lounge. I felt so bad. Shawna had come all this way to visit and have a good time, and this was what I had to offer? Nonetheless, we made it work! We sat at the bar talking and laughing and having the time of our lives! There were one or two men who tried to strike up conversations with us—mainly with her—but nothing major. We were there to enjoy each other.

Shawna started the "what about him" game—you know, the one where you point a guy out and ask your friend, "What about him?" I went along with it. It was fun! She pointed at a guy who had just walked in. He was about five two, slim, light-brown complexion. Right away I said, "*Nope!* I've had my share of short men, and I'm done with them." I couldn't figure out his outfit either. Purple shirt, white jeans, and dress shoes? Hey, to each his own, but I was *not* interested. He seemed to be by himself, but then his friend walked in. "What about him?" Shawna asked. I looked up, and standing there was this *man*. Six two, thick athletic build, chocolate complexion, handsome. The funny thing about it was that his shirt was also purple, but it worked on him. I thought that maybe they were in a fraternity. I was instantly intrigued. He piqued my interest. I had a history of making the first move, but from now on, I wanted to do things differently. I was determined not to make the first move. He and his friend welcomed two ladies who joined them. I immediately thought that they must have been on a double date, but the way he started looking at me seemed a bit too noticeable for him to be with anyone.

Shawna and I made sure to be seen. We were the only ones on the dance floor that night. I was trying to play the cat-and-mouse game, but nothing. I asked Shawna, "Why won't he just come over here and say something? It's obvious that he wants to." We noticed that they were getting ready to leave, and they were heading our way. They walked right past us. I was seriously fighting myself not to speak up and say something. As he passed me, I looked back, and so did he. We locked eyes, but he kept walking. Shawna and I sat there in disbelief. Had I made the right decision not to say anything? We talked about it the whole way home. That story was a running joke for the rest of her stay.

A few weeks later, a friend was having a birthday party at Oasis. I hadn't been there since the night with Shawna. It was the first night that it didn't snow, as we were in the late part of March. People were wall to wall. The dance floor was packed. Every table full. Thank goodness for the section reserved for birthday parties. Oasis had a level that was just a step above the ground, so I was able to get a better view of the place. I was in awe of how many people had come out. I was sort of checking for prospects too, ha ha. As I looked around, I noticed a familiar face behind the bar. I focused in only to realize it was him—the guy from the night with Shawna! If anyone was watching me, I know they were wondering what was wrong with me. I was standing there with my mouth hanging open in disbelief. I immediately pulled out my phone and called Shawna.

"*Shawna!* You won't believe who is in Oasis tonight. The guy in the purple—the chocolate one!"

"Is his friend there too?" she shrieked.

I quickly panned the room and found the short friend too. I couldn't believe it. I ran over to the guest of honor, who knew a lot of people who worked there. All she could tell me was that he was new. I had to know more. She volunteered to go get him for me. She returned, saying he would be over in a few minutes. He walked up to her, and she pointed him in my direction.

"Hi, what's your name?" I asked.

"I'm Elliott, what's your name?"

"I'm Tessa. You don't remember me?"

He quickly replied, "I don't think so. There's usually a lot of people in here, and I'm always so busy."

"Oh, okay. I see."

"I need to get back to work, but why don't you put your number in my phone and I'll call you?" Now lovers, I *never* gave out my number, but I was trying something different, so I said yes. He walked away, and I went home.

The next day my family and I were headed to Sunday dinner when my phone rang. I answered, and it was him! He asked what I was doing with the rest of my day and did I want to meet up. I was surprised. It was the most forward anyone had ever been with me. I wasn't ready to meet up, but I promised to call him later that evening. I was anxious to call him back, and we had a great conversation. We learned what we had in common, where we were from, what we were currently doing with our lives, and so forth. It was a great start to meeting someone new. I was excited. He admitted to remembering who I was from Oasis, but it hadn't hit him until after we'd exchanged numbers. I asked him about the first night we saw each other and why he didn't approach me. He said he thought we were with our boyfriends. Funny, we had been thinking the same thing. He said, "No, I was just the wingman for my friend."

"Oh, I see. Well, it's good that we're both single."

We spent the next few weeks getting to know each other. I made sure to let him know that I had been through a lot and didn't have time to waste. He said the same thing. We were both looking for a serious relationship.

Right away Elliott started showing me the things that I was missing. He was romantic—flowers for no reason, talking on the phone for hours, spending our weekends together. He was showing me some attention. I didn't ask or require much. Honesty and time were all I wanted. Lovers, I didn't know what I needed in a life partner, because I had never experienced a real partner in a relationship before. The only thing I knew was that I was looking to be equals. I wasn't taught to use a man for money or for what he could do for me. My parents worked together to reach a common goal, whatever it was.

Soon those weeks of getting to know one another led to Elliott and I deciding to make it official. It felt surreal. I hadn't carried the girlfriend title in a while. He was ready long before I was. He was aggressive with his feelings of wanting me. I didn't mind that, because the one person I wanted the most had never showed me he wanted me. My parents were anxious to meet the "man behind the flowers." That's what they called him, because he bought me flowers so often. It was Easter weekend, and my parents had dinner at our house. I invited Elliott to come and meet my family before our date. He didn't shy away. He was eager and willing. He displayed so much confidence in his actions toward me. He was strong—strong-willed and strong-minded. I needed a man to show me that he wasn't afraid to be with me. He wasn't making time to entertain any other females. He wanted me and only me. April 2011 was the beginning of a new life.

Chapter 9
Bros Before Who?

The year 2011 was also the year that things started to take off for Chase. Although his dream was to play in the NFL, he was offered a contract to play arena football. He had met the love of his life, Farrah, and they were as happy as could be. Everything was falling into place for him. Chase had a lot to celebrate. He was throwing a big party, and he wanted everyone there. I remember talking on the phone with Marie while getting dressed for the party, and Chase called.

"Hey, what's up, Chase?"

"Hey, Tess. I invited Jesse, is that cool?"

My heart sank. I was both pissed off and hurt at the same time. "Um, no, but what can I do about it?"

"I wasn't sure if everything was cool between you guys or not, so I just wanted to give you the heads-up."

"Yeah, okay, sure." I just hung up. So many thoughts started to flood my mind. How did I look? Should I say something to Elliott? I had already given him some background on the situation with Jesse and me. After all, almost everything that made me into the person I was relationship-wise was because of Jesse. I started judging everything about myself—I look overweight, I'm too dark from the sun, my hair isn't done right. I couldn't even look at myself in the mirror. Lovers, how could I let someone who made me feel so worthless even affect my mentality that way? I hadn't seen or talked to him in three years. Why the hell was he even going to be there? I was so angry. My eyes started to fill up, and tears started to fall. How could Chase do this to me? We were like siblings. I trusted him. Why was he still friends with Jesse after he broke my heart? What the hell was going on that I didn't know about? So many questions would go unanswered, because I couldn't address them at the party, and I didn't want to look like a fool for even caring. I had already expressed how I felt about the two of them, so if he chose to continue a friendship with Jesse, there was no way Chase cared for me the way I thought he did—or the way he should. I took every feeling I had and stuffed it down. I had to put on a pretty face for everyone around me. I couldn't let Elliott see me upset, I couldn't ruin the party for Chase, and I had to look happy to Jesse. Talk about feeling uncomfortable.

 Elliott and I arrived at the party. Not too many people were there yet, but there were enough people to go around and say hello. As much as I was trying not to, I was already looking around the room anxiously to find Jesse. I spotted him sitting at the far bar. Elliott and I spoke to all my family who were there. I said a few hellos to Chase's friends. The answer to your burning question, lovers, is no! I did not walk up to Jesse and say hello. I noticed when he turned around; I'm not sure what he was looking for, but I waved from a distance, and he waved back with a smile. He was alone. I suddenly had mixed feelings. I didn't know how seeing him would make me feel. I felt like the biggest fraud. I felt so many emotions, but I had to express the happy ones and only those. Jesse had to see that I had moved on and couldn't care less.

Every single party that Chase and Farrah had, Jesse was there. I overheard Chase say that Jesse was his agent. It made sense. It all added up, but I still couldn't figure out why. Of all the athletes and agents out there, why had they chosen each other? Why didn't either of them choose me? Each and every time we saw each other, we would wave hello, and that was it. Extremely weird, I know. So awkward. The awkwardness never got any easier.

Chapter 10
Bells and Babies

All I could do was focus on my relationship with Elliott. Time waits for no man, and I wasn't getting any younger. I wanted to get married and have a family. Elliott felt the same way. After dating for a year, Elliott popped the question, and I accepted! I know what you're thinking—one year isn't long enough to make such a big decision. But it was very simple. Neither of us had children, we weren't interested in being with anyone else, we weren't playing games, and we wanted the same things. His family was small; his mom had worked hard to take care of him and his twin brother. He was happy to be accepted in a large, loving family. We took a year to plan the wedding and were married in July 2013.

We didn't waste any time on starting a family. We found out in November 2013 that we were expecting! I was so excited to become a mom. Being a mom was literally my life's dream. Our due date was July 11, 2014! The day Elliott and I went to our first ultrasound, I was about twelve weeks. We were so excited! The tech came in, took a bunch of pictures, and went out to get the doctor. The doctor came in and said, "Can you see on the monitor that there's no red color around the baby? That means the baby has passed on. I'm so sorry."

Hit hard with devastation, Elliott and I looked at each other with confusion and sadness. I instantly started crying. The doctor told us to take our time and gather ourselves, then meet her in her office. We had to discuss the next steps. I knew everyone was waiting for us to come back with pictures and updates, so I turned my phone off. I didn't want to tell anyone the news until I was ready. Meanwhile both Farrah and Elliott's sister-in-law were expecting. Elliott and I were so hurt. The doctor said I could take a pill to pass the pregnancy, or I could have a procedure. Once I told my mother, she suggested that I have the procedure, and that's what I did. Why did we have to lose our baby? I tried to obey my parents and God. Why was I being punished? It was the hardest thing I ever had to do, but God got us through. After coming through the procedure, we stopped trying. We needed time to process what we'd gone through and how to prevent it from happening again, if possible.

September 2014, I woke Elliott out of his sleep with a positive pregnancy test in my hand, tears flowing—happy tears, of course, with a little fear. We decided right then and there that we weren't going to tell anyone. Last time we'd told the whole world, which only made it harder on us to have to tell them all about the miscarriage. We held onto the news until after the first trimester. All the appointments were good. The heartbeat was strong at every single visit. My parents went with me to the first ultrasound since Elliott couldn't get off work in time. When we entered the room, I was overcome with emotion as I recalled the last time I was in this exact same situation a year before. The technician asked if I had ever had an ultrasound before. I replied yes. He put the gel on my baby bump and then the scope and said, "Did they tell you that you're having two?"

What? I looked up at the monitor, and there they were. Both of our little angels. My mom almost fainted, and my dad said, "I knew it!" I laughed so hard. I was so happy, and I couldn't believe it. God hadn't just given us one baby; he'd given us two! We later found out we were having identical twin girls!

The journey was long and hard at times but blessed. Lovers, by week thirty I could barely walk. I was using a wheelchair whenever I went out. My entire body was swollen. I didn't want to be seen at all. I was huge. My niece's birthday party was just two weeks before I was due to deliver. Chase and Farrah's daughter was turning one. A part of me wanted to use the pregnancy as an excuse not to show up, but I didn't want to be that way. I still didn't want to see Jesse though. I decided to text Chase and ask him if he had invited Jesse, and he said yes. This was the moment it all became clear that my feelings didn't matter one bit to Chase. We literally got into an argument over it. My only point was that I felt it wasn't a place for Jesse to be, mainly because I didn't want him to see me. I know what you're thinking: Why would I care about anyone seeing me as a woman who was carrying not one but two precious lives in her womb? How could I make a child's birthday party about me? My judgment was clouded by my emotions, and I realize I was wrong, but the way I see it, every time Chase invited Jesse to be in my presence, he was wrong too. Anyway, I only wanted Jesse to see me at my absolute best. Chase felt I was being unreasonable, and he let me know the party was about his daughter and that everyone in attendance was coming to celebrate her. I tried talking to my mom about it, but she felt the same way as Chase. Who cares about an ex being around? I tried expressing that it wasn't just uncomfortable for me but that it had to be uncomfortable for my husband as well. This wasn't just an ex; Jesse was *the* ex. I even tried expressing to my husband how I felt, but he didn't seem to understand why I cared. I know my reasons didn't make much sense, because I couldn't just yell out, "I never got over what we were. I still struggle with it. My heart breaks every time I see his face," I'm sure that would have made things a little easier to understand, but what man wants to hear his wife say those words? I had to let it go.

 The day of the party arrived. It was the coolest party for a one-year-old that I'd ever seen with my own eyes. The party was on the basement level of the venue, so getting from the car to the building and into the actual party would have been impossible without the wheelchair. I didn't want to bring any attention to myself, but I was hard to miss. I was over two hundred pounds. The only place the wheelchair would fit was near the food table. So many people came to say hello and ask about my pregnancy. I kept it together. I even managed to wave hello to Jesse, still from a distance. He was alone as usual. Chase was having the time of his life at the party, celebrating his firstborn child. I didn't expect there to be any tension, not from him at least. Sure, I had some, but I didn't show it. I couldn't. I would have been the guilty one or the one who was overreacting.

Easter Sunday 2015 was the day my doctor wanted me to report to the hospital to be induced. There were special circumstances that meant the twins had to be delivered no later than thirty-seven weeks. After thirty-two hours of labor and never reaching ten centimeters' dilation, they wheeled me back for a C-section. The girls were born at 2:36 a.m. Chase visited while we were in the hospital. His presence meant a lot, because we were still close, despite the recent shift in our relationship. A conversation came up about all the people he knew who had recently had children. He mentioned Jesse had had his second child back in February. I didn't realize we had gotten to that point. To be honest, I *wasn't* at that point. I didn't want to discuss Jesse and his life in our conversations. I felt like I had to brush it under the rug, though, so I just said, "Aww, really?" The subject changed quickly. Maybe he was trying to see how I would react. It was weird. Chase and I discussing Jesse was not something I was interested in. In any

Harmony Lynn

case, Elliott and I took our baby girls home five days later, and life was never the same—in a good way!

Chapter 11
R.I.P. Anthony

Chase was out on the road for the rest of the year, which meant no parties and no Jesse. Life was going fine, but then tragedy struck. I woke up early one morning to a phone call from Marie, telling me that Anthony had been shot and killed.

I was shocked. "Wait, what? Ant, Jesse's best friend? No way."

"Yes," she replied. "I saw it all over Facebook and Instagram."

I couldn't believe it. I actually started crying. It had been years since I'd spoken with Anthony, but we followed each other on social media, and he was always my biggest fan when it came to Jesse. Oh my God—Jesse. Was he okay? He must be devastated right now. I was always good for checking in on Jesse when I thought he needed me, but when you go years without speaking to someone, you're not exactly sure how to proceed. Reaching out to him was on my mind all day at work. I even asked a friend at work what I should do. I decided to reach out but keep it simple. Jesse had had the same cell phone number since high school, and I had it memorized. The message read: Hey Jesse, it's Tessa. I heard about Anthony, and I'm so sorry for your loss. I will keep you and the guys in my prayers. He replied: Thank you.

As crazy as it sounds, all I wanted to do was run to him. Never mind the bitterness I carried. Never mind the anger I had for his friendship with my cousin. Nothing matters when you lose a loved one. You realize life is too short to sweat the small things. None of that mattered now. Jesse had just lost his best friend. I had to support him during such a devastating time in his life. I wasn't sure what would come of that single text message I sent, but it didn't matter. I just wanted him to know that I was there for him.

Lovers, try not to be angry with me, because I was acting from a place in my heart that I tried to hide for so many years. I know it was wrong of me. I was a married woman with a family. My actions were not okay, especially when my husband didn't know anything about it. A friend from high school reached out, saying she would attend the funeral with me. I was nervous. Attending a funeral is a part of life that no one really wants to go through, but it's a time to show support and love to those who need it. I couldn't bring myself to even view Anthony. I stayed in my seat. I wanted to speak to Jesse and hug him, but I just wasn't sure how he'd react. It was a beautiful service, and I hope Anthony was resting peacefully in heaven while watching over his friends and family celebrate his life.

A few weeks had passed, and Jesse was heavy on my mind. I wanted to contact him, so I justified my actions. I thought, what's the harm in reaching out to someone to check on them? There was nothing going on between us, so why would it matter? I sent a text saying: Hi, how are you? He answered that he was doing okay. I told him if he needed to talk, he could always talk to me. He appreciated me saying that.

There was a certain comfort I got from communicating with him. From there our text conversations became more frequent. Sometimes he would text first, which made me feel like the feeling was mutual. I am not saying it was a romantic feeling, but it was something. It was like catching up with an old friend. Most of our conversations were about something funny from our pasts. It was a walk down memory lane. I couldn't help but throw in some ugly truths every now and again though. For instance, I apologized for being too overbearing. I thought if I showed him that I could be everything to him, he would want me, but that was too much and definitely too soon. I was obsessed. It's embarrassing to even say that, but it's true. When he broke his leg, I cooked, made a cake, and made a homemade card. We were like sixteen and seventeen. The expression "doing too much" wasn't out then, but I was the definition! In hindsight, I see I was being taken advantage of. I can't recall a single thing Jesse ever did for me besides show his face. I think that I was the laughingstock for him and his friends, but it was water under the bridge. I couldn't help but ask what had pushed him away. He said he was young and intimidated, but I couldn't figure out how I could have intimidated him. Sure, I was a little older, but I was the one who'd initiated what we had. His answer wasn't the one I was expecting, and it wasn't the answer I believed.

Unfortunately, sometimes we make up what we want to believe, and even hearing something different directly from a person's mouth can't change it. I needed him to be brutally honest. I had spent so much time convincing myself that it was me, that there was something about me that he just didn't like. My complexion, my body type, our chemistry or lack thereof, something I did or something I said. But no. He said it was the fact that he was young and intimidated. In my mind I wondered, if that was the truth, then why hadn't he come back to me when he'd grown up enough to admit it? For some reason I always thought that in the end it would be us. Clearly, he had already let that go.

Chapter 12
Wait, What?

It wasn't long before the conversation shifted to our relationships.

I texted: Are you happy, Jesse?

Yeah.

So that's wifey, then?

That's the plan, but who knows when.

How much does she know about me?

Nothing. How much does he know?

A lot.

Elliott knew things about my relationship with Jesse that Jesse didn't even know.

Are you happy, Tess?

It's complicated.

Elliott and I were going through a rough patch. Lovers, marriage is hard work. Really hard. There were so many things that I didn't even think about before getting married. So many things that I hadn't done as an individual to better myself. So many things that we didn't know about each other, but it was my fault. When you're so focused on making sure you find love, you forget about the other important elements of a relationship that you need just as much as love, like clear communication, mental stimulation, intellectual conversation, and intimacy that doesn't involve sex. I searched for someone who was going to love me, really love me, and I found that. However, I realize that my controlling ways caused me to move more quickly than I should have. That being said, I believe that God is in control of all things, and if he allowed me to take the big life steps that I took, then it was for a reason. However, I wish I would've done the work to really know who I was, what I wanted, and what I needed in my life.

When I told Jesse it was complicated, he sent back a sad-face emoji and said: Do you want to talk about it? Because I don't like complicated.

I could have said so many things. I wanted to talk about it, but not via text. That's not talking. But at the same time, when you talk to another man about the issues you have with your man, it's a sign that something is really wrong. Not to mention these two men had been in each other's presence on numerous occasions. They were both close with Chase, so the *play it cool* act was something they both felt they had to do. Watching them speak to each other and hold conversations made my skin crawl. I just told him maybe some other time.

Now, lovers, maybe you can help me understand the behavior of this man, because I stayed confused. We were the best of friends when we texted during the day. You know, those hours that you know someone isn't around their significant other. Then when we would hang out with Chase, Jesse would only say hello. I just felt like, there's nothing going on here. We're literally catching up. The next day he would be the first to text and reference something from the night before. I was cool with it at first, but then it became weird. Now, I didn't expect for us to sit together and carry on a conversation, because that would have looked suspicious, but I felt like we could say more than hello. I think he was nervous. Jesse wasn't a confrontational person, nor did he want to do anything that would cause a problem with anyone. He loved to say, "I don't want to cause problems in your household."

My response was always, "You can only cause a problem if I allow you to." He tried to talk more, but it just kept returning to text conversations. It was an awkward situation either way, so I didn't trip about it.

I honestly can't remember how this particular conversation started, but he stated that I'd changed my number a few times and gone missing on him. I asked, "Why did that matter? Were you looking for me?"

He answered, "I'm never not." Lovers! Oh my God, those three words held so much weight. For him to say he was always looking for me meant so much to me. Maybe, I thought, just maybe, somewhere way deep down, he loved me and always had. So much time had passed, and it was true, I had changed my number a lot. He didn't have my number until I reached out about Anthony. I joked that he'd gone off and had a baby on me before I even met my husband. He said that I'd gone off and gotten married and changed my last name, which he hadn't done. I told him just because he wasn't married, that didn't change the dynamic of his relationship with his girlfriend, which was just like being married. They had three children and lived together. He kept repeating that he hadn't married her yet though. I wondered why. If she was everything he'd ever wanted and they had children together, why wait? But I didn't pry. That issue was between him and the mother of his children.

To me, his actions alluded to one thing, but he couldn't bring himself to say the words. Now let's be clear: if he wanted to admit that I was his person and he loved me from the bottom of his heart, I could have taken that in and accepted it for what it was. I would not have expected for us to blow up our relationships based on feelings from a decade ago. I would've wanted to see his face and hear those words come out of his mouth. I told him that some of the things he said made me feel like he wanted to say more to me, so why not just say it? But then I asked him to refrain. In the midst of all of this, and with the uncertainty of my marriage, I wanted to make sure that his words weren't going to influence any of my decisions. I knew that I needed to stop talking to him. I never thought that I'd have anything to do with him again, but life showed me to never say never. Our conversations would come to a screeching halt before I knew it, though, lovers.

Elliott and I decided to start having these weekly conversations about our marriage: what we liked, what we didn't like, what we felt was lacking. One Sunday night during our conversation, he said that he'd seen something in my phone that was strange. I have no idea when he had time to go through my phone or if he noticed it while sitting beside me. He said he saw a picture of Jesse that I thought I'd deleted. He said he didn't know that we were talking outside of the events involving Chase and that I must think he looked good if I wanted his picture. I was trying to be as honest as I could. Yes, I told him, I think he's attractive. As far as our conversations, I let him know how it started. He didn't understand, or at least he tried to pretend he didn't.

I wasn't intentionally trying to cause any pain; I just wanted to be honest with myself about my own feelings. He went on to say how disrespectful Jesse was to think he would tolerate such behavior behind his back. I apologized for my behavior, and I admitted that I was wrong. But now I felt that I had put a target on Jesse's back without him knowing it, so I felt that I should give him a heads-up. When I told Jesse about my husband's discovery, he panicked! Jesse didn't even remember what pictures he had sent. He said how he didn't want to cause any problems, and again I had to explain that the problem wasn't that he'd sent me a picture but that I'd kept it. The problem was that I had even asked for it. The problem was me, not him.

Once I let Jesse know that he was a topic of discussion between me and my husband, he went silent. No texts, barely speaking when we saw each other. So I decided to text him something light and comical, nothing too serious.

You acting funny or nah?

He replied with the laughing emojis, saying, Look what happened last time.

Oh, so you are acting funny.

I'm just trying to let you be great.

I don't know why, but that response pissed me off! Let me be great? He did not have the power to *let* me be anything. I said, Oh, okay, and I left it all right there. I didn't text anymore, and I completely avoided him at all costs when we were around each other. I slowly returned to being upset that he was even around. He still showed up just like the rest of the family. If Chase was having the *family* over, that always meant Jesse and his family would be there. His kids playing with my kids, all the guys—including my husband—sitting around talking and laughing, walking past each other from room to room. The awkwardness was back and at an all-time high. You could have cut the tension with a knife.

Chapter 13
So Awkward

Can you imagine your ex walking into your family gathering with *his* family? Sitting around looking so comfortable, as if *you* are the one who's out of place? The shit was so aggravating. I mean, when you break it down, Chase and I were like brother and sister, and all his friends call me Sis, but Jesse could never call me that. I could hold a conversation with everyone in the room except for him. Our avoidance was becoming noticeable to those around us. My mother was the first to make a comment that I must've told him not to talk to me, because he would go the other way to avoid me also. I told her no, his actions were all on him. Now, lovers, get this. My husband said it was weird that we didn't speak. *What?* How was it weird? Just a few months ago, Elliott didn't want me to talk to Jesse, but now it was weird that I didn't? Jesse and I were literally walking past each other and not even making eye contact, which took even more energy to do. I was over it. Since this was a part of life that had been forced upon me, and it wasn't going to change, I needed to accept it so that my life didn't feel so strained.

Chase and Farrah always wanted to have the family over. I tried desperately to skip out. I always wanted to just stay home and make better use of my time. But my mother was not going for it. Her favorite line was, "Sunday is family day, and you need to come be around your family." I made sure to say that Chase was good for inviting people who weren't family, and I didn't always feel like being bothered. She said that his friends were family to him. Exactly, Mother. He'd rather have them than have me. A total male chauvinist. Jesse showed up as if his life depended on it. The way I see it, Jesse worked for Chase. They were going to have a business relationship no matter what. If he didn't show up to the family gatherings, he'd still have a job, and they'd still be friends. I, on the other hand, had to show up because Mom said so and because I was actually family. Here I was again, forced to take my feelings and stuff them down my own throat. No one cared. I felt alone and unprotected. All I wanted was for someone to say they understood where I was coming from and to agree that Chase was wrong.

Chapter 14
Marital Bliss

I won't lie to you, lovers. When I quit talking to Jesse, my marriage got better. We weren't arguing as much. We were talking more. We were making future plans. We were talking about having more children. We were hopeful. We went to therapy, and we prayed together. Things were looking up. We had to do everything we could to try and save our marriage, because letting it go would've been the easy part. God turned it around for us. It amazed me how much of a 180-degree turnaround we did. Our talk about having another child soon became a reality. We found out that we were expecting a few days before Chase and Farrah's wedding weekend. The wedding was an intimate ceremony with their closest friends and family. Yes, Jesse was a groomsman. He and Chase had become brothers. That's what they called each other. They posted things on social media like, "Happy birthday to my brother" and "Congratulations to my bro." That would always sound crazy to me, but whatever.

The night of the rehearsal dinner, just before things kicked off, I had this weird feeling. I was spotting. As much as I tried to hold back the tears, they just started rolling. Elliott and I had been through this before, and while spotting means nothing for some women, it meant that something was wrong in my case. I didn't stay at the party long. I grabbed up the girls and went back to the hotel. The bleeding got heavier, so I called the nurse line, and they suggested that I go to the closest emergency room. The next morning, which was Chase's wedding day, I got up early and headed to the ER. They took blood and did a pregnancy test. The test was still coming back positive, but the bleeding was still happening. The ER doctor explained that they would be looking to see if my Human Chorionic Gonadotropin (HCG) levels were going up or down. If they were going down, then I was losing the pregnancy. I wouldn't get the results back until after the wedding, so I had to be a big girl and get through the rest of the festivities. I didn't tell anyone that I was going to the ER, just my husband. I told everyone else that I was running some errands. As I pulled up to the front of the hotel to valet-park the car, I looked up to see the groom and his *brother* Jesse standing outside. I thought, "Can I catch a break? Now I have to hide this hospital bracelet, I look a little crazy, and I can't even avoid them." I made it quick—"Hey, good morning, where are you guys headed? Oh, okay, see you at the altar!" I hated moments like that. I hated feeling like the oddball when I was the one who was truly family to Chase. I hated knowing that he and Jesse had become closer than Chase and I could ever be. I had literally lost my cousin, who was like a brother to me, to my ex.

Going through a miscarriage in the midst of Chase's wedding weekend celebration was tough. The miscarriage itself is sad; it's hard, it's confusing, and it's painful, but I had to find the silver lining. I had something else going on that I could use as a distraction, and this time the doctors didn't have to go in and get my baby. I passed the pregnancy on my own. Thank God for his blessings. It could've been a lot worse.

Per the doctor's orders, we waited a few months before trying again. During the wait I started taking a prenatal vitamin and a folic acid pill every day. Apparently when certain things are missing or low in my body while trying to conceive, I miscarry. We would soon learn that we were expecting again, and this would be our fourth time. We waited to tell anyone, of course. At my eight-week appointment, the midwife said, "I can see the heartbeat here on the monitor, which usually means the pregnancy is healthy." I was excited! I called Elliott and told him about the appointment once I left. No, he didn't go with me, but I wasn't going to let it bother me. I was carrying a precious life in my womb—that was all I cared about.

Once the first trimester was over, we started making announcements. My aunts said they already knew. I was definitely showing. It wasn't long before it was time to find out the gender. I went by myself, but I didn't look. I had them print out the results, and I gave the envelope to my Aunt Candice, who put together an entire gender reveal party at my parents' house. Pink and blue everywhere! Games, food, and fun. It was hard to wait for the big reveal, but it was worth the wait. When my Aunt dropped the balloons over our heads, the crowd went wild—we were having a baby boy! It didn't matter to me what the gender was; after experiencing two miscarriages, all I wanted was a healthy baby to love for life. God gave us just that. Our son was born a few months later and I fell in love all over again.

The time was flying by. Our girls were a few months younger than Jesse's youngest son, who was turning four. Chase and Farrah's daughter, who would soon be five, was invited to the party. Farrah asked me if my girls could come along too. I didn't know how to answer. How weird and awkward would it be to show up uninvited? Farrah insisted that Jesse had said anyone could come. I didn't believe it. He had my number, but he hadn't sent me an invite. My husband was acting like it was all good. He kept asking me if I wanted to take the girls. I said no over and over. I wanted to text Jesse and ask him, but who asks to be invited to a children's party?

We decided to take the kids to an activity gym instead. They were fine with that. I had an uneasy feeling though. Would this really be the next phase of this Jesse business—we have to do kids' party invites? We have to start inviting each other to personal events that we're having in an effort to be normal? Will this ever be normal? Needless to say, I was over it, but I knew I needed to clear the air with Jesse. It was getting too thick and too uncomfortable for me. He and my husband were still carrying on conversations that I hated to witness, but Jesse and I didn't say a word to each other. Not even a hello sometimes. It was time for me to be the bigger person. Time for me to initiate a conversation that wasn't through text.

Chapter 15
Clearing the Air

The amount of time that passed since Jesse and I had spoken allowed me to be very honest with myself about so much, lovers. I realized that while I may have loved him deeply, he was not my person. He would never be able to love me the way I wanted to be loved. He was selfish, and that characteristic wouldn't be good in a relationship. He wasn't as honest and open as I needed him to be. And I wasn't his person either. I wasn't his type. I wasn't beautiful enough for him. I wasn't enough for him. I had watched him pursue every female he'd ever wanted. Not actually watched, but you get what I'm saying. Any woman he wanted, he found a way to get her. But he never pursued me. I pursued him, and it all started for clout. He was an underclassman who was being sought after by an upperclassman. He was the man for that reason alone. He got more than he bargained for, I'm sure. I was trying to be too much to someone who didn't want to be much of anything at all for me. If he did want to, he never said it and never really showed it. I admit that I don't think an adult relationship would actually work between Jesse and me, if it were an option. I learned what I need in a relationship, and I don't believe Jesse can provide what I need.

I am a lot to handle, too much sometimes. I had to come to terms with knowing that our history didn't matter. I would've wanted him to be family by marriage, but instead he chose to be family by friendship with Chase. I couldn't figure out why Jesse would want to be family with my family. He had to know that I would be present at every gathering Chase had. Why would he choose to become brothers with Chase, knowing I would be around? Did he do it on purpose? Maybe he hoped that we would work it out one day. I intended to get answers. I reached out and let him know that I wanted to get rid of the awkwardness and just move on. He agreed to have a talk with me. I thought it'd be best to speak over the phone, because I didn't think my husband would go for me saying, "I'm going to go see Jesse so we can talk this thing out." I would've preferred to speak in person, though, because it would have been harder for him to lie to my face. I wanted him to see my face and how bothered I was by the choices both he and Chase had made. But I settled for the phone call.

One thing that has never changed about Jesse is his ability to keep everything lighthearted. He was always smiling and laughing. I think that was always his way to lighten the seriousness of a situation. I wasn't too serious, but I wasn't very upbeat either. I was dreading the conversation, because I already knew how it would end. I let him speak his peace. He said that things were definitely awkward when we were around each other. I let him know that people were starting to notice. I explained to him that when he responded as if texting each other was too much, I just figured he didn't want me to say anything to him, so I quit all communication. As usual, he said he didn't want to cause problems in my household. I explained for the final time that if he was pursuing me, and I was clearly bothered by it, only then would it be a problem. However, I was an equal participant in our exchange, and therefore I was the problem. A person can only go as far as you let them. I told him that I was guilty of changing my number and *going missing*, but while I was doing that, I had no way of knowing that he and Chase were off becoming *brothers*.

"Why, Jesse?" I asked. "You knew that you would run into me eventually. No two people who were once together have to deal with one another once the relationship ends unless they have children together. But thanks to you, we have an entire awkward situation."

"It just happened. I didn't even think about it like that, for real."

Talk about twisting the knife, lovers. After going back and forth with someone for over ten years, you become best friends with her cousin, and you never think about her or how she may feel about it one time? There it was, folks. The last confirmation that he'd never given a damn about me. I let him know that I was still holding on to something that he'd let go of long before I did. I let him know that I'd told Chase how I felt as well, but boys will be boys, right? Neither of them considered my feelings at all.

I asked him to take accountability for his part in misleading me.

With a high-pitched voice, he said, *"Me?"*

"Yes, you."

"How?" he asked.

"Accusing me of going missing and getting married on you and saying that you're always looking for me. Why would you say that?"

He seemed to be struggling with his words. "To check on you and make sure that you were good," he said. The tone in his voice just didn't sound like he was telling the truth.

"So you check on everybody then, right?"

"No."

"Then why say that to me?"

"I didn't mean it like that."

"Well, Jesse, look, I don't know how many other women you might be carrying on conversations with, but please be careful what you say, because women can take certain things you say the wrong way. I cannot handle gray areas; it has to be black and white. I wasn't clear before, but I am clear now."

I had said all I needed to say. We agreed to speak to one another when we saw each other, and that was it. Nothing more, nothing less.

Chapter 16
Over It—Like, for Real

Closure. Something that I thought I had years ago. I felt a little better, but it still felt awkward. I can honestly say that I am *finally* over him. Over the emotional abuse. Over feeling inferior to him or his *type*. I am enough. I am beautiful. I am worthy to be loved, and so are you. Lovers, you may have a history with someone, and you might think that history will always outweigh any obstacles the two of you will face. This may be true for some people, but if you have any doubt, any gut feelings that you are wasting your time, run. Gather what's left of your broken heart, your hurt feelings, your self-esteem, and go. It's time to heal. It's time to find the love that will help you flourish. You are allowed to change your requirements and expectations of whom you choose to be with. It's a part of growth. No one stays the same forever. You don't have to live for anyone else but yourself. Don't be ashamed about fully loving someone. Don't feel stupid. When you take a step back, you will suddenly realize how much you've learned from that person. You will see how much you learned about yourself.

I want you to learn from me and my mistakes. Take your time and find out what love truly is *for you*. It is not sex, it is not abuse, it is not material things, it is not a person with good looks. Love should always make you feel respected in times of disagreement and grateful in times of anger. A relationship is not always going to be smooth sailing. I think love is what you want and need it to be. Only you can determine the type of love you need. Only you know what you require from the person you choose to love. I used to think that love was very simple: two people spend time together, have common interests and morals, and eventually they develop romantic feelings for one another. I used to think that was enough. No, lovers. It is not. Love is so much deeper than that. At least for me. You will have to put yourself out there to find it, but when you do, it's worth it. There will be rough times. In those rough times, if you can't recall why you chose them, you have to figure out how to face the hard truth and determine what you need to do next. It may take time to know what you need, but once you know, don't ever stop being honest and up front about it. If you're not, you'll only end up hurting yourself. Choose yourself, love yourself, and take care of your heart like your life depends on it.

Break free from any love that doesn't make you feel amazing about yourself, lovers. I am so glad that I am free from the burden of loving the wrong person and that Elliott came along to show me what love really is. I am healing and I am free.